For Odette, Massi, Lorenzo
and, of course, Federica

Groundwood Books / House of Anansi Press
groundwoodbooks.com

We acknowledge for their financial support of our publishing program the Canada Council for
the Arts, the Ontario Arts Council and the Government of Canada.

 Canada Council   Conseil des Arts
for the Arts   du Canada

 ONTARIO ARTS COUNCIL
CONSEIL DES ARTS DE L'ONTARIO
an Ontario government agency
un organisme du gouvernement de l'Ontario

 With the participation of the Government of Canada   Canadä
Avec la participation du gouvernement du Canada

Library and Archives Canada Cataloguing in Publication
Ritchie, Scot author, illustrator
Federica / Scot Ritchie.
Issued in print and electronic formats.
ISBN 978-1-55498-968-3 (hardcover). — ISBN 978-1-55498-969-0 (PDF)
I. Title.
PS8635.I825F43 2017   jC813'.6   C2016-908001-3
C2016-908002-1

The illustrations were rendered in ink and Adobe Photoshop.
Design by Michael Solomon
Printed and bound in Malaysia

33614080541096

FSC
www.fsc.org

MIX
Paper from
responsible sources
FSC® C012700

Federica

SCOT RITCHIE

GROUNDWOOD BOOKS
HOUSE OF ANANSI PRESS
Toronto   Berkeley

On the edge of a big city, in a medium-sized house, lived a little girl named Federica. Her mum and dad were always too busy to tidy up, so her house was a buggy, buzzy mess.

To get away from it all, Federica would go to the park, where everything was peaceful.

Federica loved spending time with all the creatures in the park. And one day she had an idea.

First, Federica asked the sheep and goats to come with her.

"Can my friends come in?" she asked. "They're a bit woolly."

Her dad was busy trimming a tree into the shape of a donut.

"Uh-huh," he said.

Federica led them up to her bedroom.
"Baaah!"

Federica ran back to the park to get some spiders and dragonflies. "Can my friends come in? They eat flies."

"Of course, dear!" said her mother.
Federica led the way to her bedroom. The
dragonflies zoomed ahead, as the spiders walked up
the stairs on their long thin legs.
She closed her bedroom door.

Federica talked to a toad and an owl.
"I have mice," she said, and they both
followed her home.
"*Hoot!*"
"*Croak!*"
"That's nice, dear," Mum answered
without looking up.

The owl swooped upstairs and settled on Federica's bedside lamp, while the toad hopped into her hat and fell asleep.

Federica brought back some raccoons.

"My friends eat garbage!" Federica yelled. "Can they come in?"

"Of course, dear," said Dad.

Now the bedroom was full. It was time for the second part of her plan.

"Can we go to the park for a picnic?"
asked Federica.

"What a nice idea!" said Mum as she
brushed a fly from the baby's nose.

Federica's mother packed blankets and games, while her father prepared some food.

"As soon as you hear the front door close, come out!" whispered Federica.

As soon as they heard the door close, the animals poured out of the bedroom and spread through the house.

The sheep ran to the backyard to enjoy the long green grass, while the goats gobbled up the leaves on the carpet. Spiders started making webs. The toad hopped down the hall after a moth. The raccoons ate up the garbage and then started cleaning dishes.

The family enjoyed their day
at the park.

It was late, time to go home.
Federica was so excited she had to
pull her hat down to distract herself.

"There is a raccoon in my kitchen," said Mum.
"There's a sheep asleep in my jeep!" said Dad.

"But look!" said Federica.
Everything had changed.
The flies were gone, the carpet was clean.
The grass was cut, and the kitchen spotless.
Federica's plan had worked.

A few days later though, Federica realized that her friends might be better off back in their real homes.

So they all went back to the park.
And Federica visited them every day.

But not until family cleanup hour was done.